My First Collection of Songs

PaRragon

Bath · New York · Singapore · Hong Kong · Cologne · Delhi · Melbourne

Hey, diddle, diddle

Hey, diddle, diddle, the cat and the fiddle,
The cow jumped over the moon;
The little dog laughed to see such sport
And the dish ran away with the spoon.

5

Twinkle,
twinkle, little star

Twinkle, twinkle, little star,
How I wonder what you are!
Up above the world so high,
Like a diamond in the sky.
Twinkle, twinkle, little star,
How I wonder what you are!

7

It's raining, it's pouring

It's raining, it's pouring,
The old man's snoring;
He went to bed and bumped his head
And couldn't get up in the morning.

9

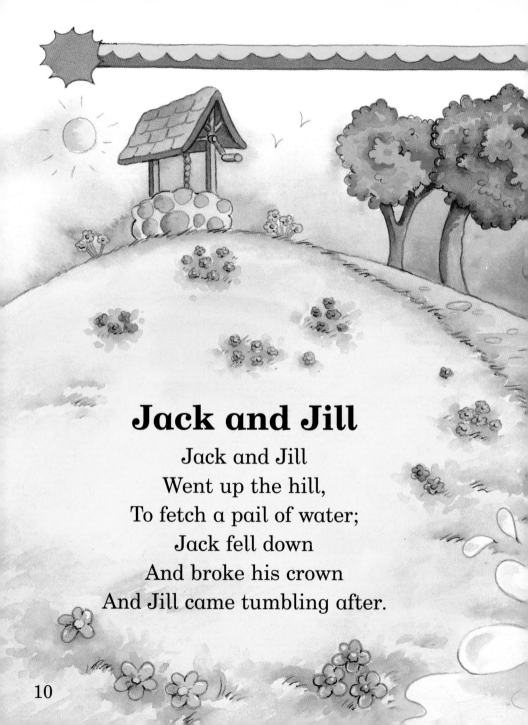

Jack and Jill

Jack and Jill
Went up the hill,
To fetch a pail of water;
Jack fell down
And broke his crown
And Jill came tumbling after.

11

See-saw, Margery Daw

See-saw, Margery Daw,
Johnny shall have a new master;

He shall have, but a penny a day,
Because he can't work any faster.

13

Hickory, dickory, dock

Hickory, dickory, dock,
The mouse ran up the clock.
The clock struck one,
The mouse ran down,
Hickory, dickory, dock.

14

Pat-a-cake, pat-a-cake

Pat-a-cake, pat-a-cake, baker's man,
Bake me a cake as fast as you can;
Pat it and prick it and mark it with B
And put it in the oven for baby and me.

Mary, Mary, quite contrary

Mary, Mary, quite contrary,
How does your garden grow?
With silver bells and cockle shells
And pretty maids all in a row.

Simple Simon

Simple Simon met a pieman,
Going to the fair;
Said Simple Simon to the pieman,
Let me taste your ware.

21

Three blind mice

Three blind mice, see how they run!
They all ran after the farmer's wife,
Who cut off their tails with a carving knife.
Did you ever see such a thing in your life,
As three blind mice?

22

23

Baa, baa, black sheep

Baa, baa, black sheep,
Have you any wool?
Yes, sir, yes, sir, three bags full;

One for the master
And one for the dame
And one for the little boy,
Who lives down the lane.

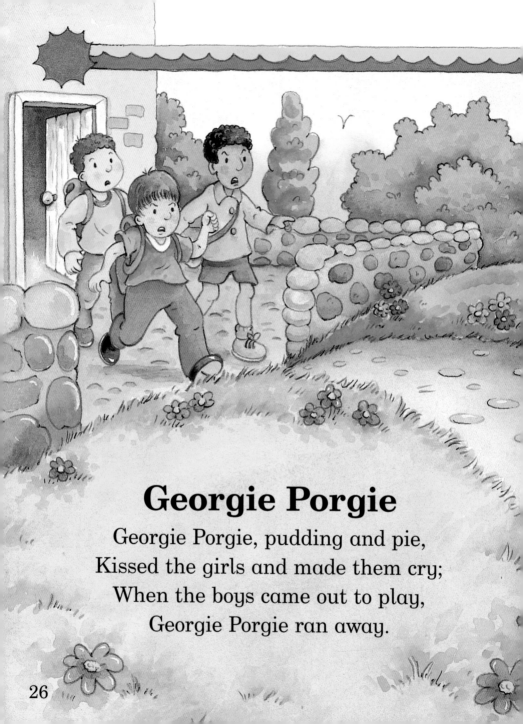

Georgie Porgie

Georgie Porgie, pudding and pie,
Kissed the girls and made them cry;
When the boys came out to play,
Georgie Porgie ran away.

27

Hush-a-bye, baby

Hush-a-bye, baby, on the tree top,
When the wind blows, the cradle will rock;
When the bough breaks, the cradle will fall,
Down will come baby, cradle and all.